Snow Puppies

By Barbara Bazaldua
Illustrated by Don Williams

A GOLDEN BOOK • NEW YORK
Golden Books Publishing Company, Inc., Racine, Wisconsin 53404

© 1996 Disney Enterprises, Inc. Based on the book by Dodie Smith, published by Viking Press.
All rights reserved. Printed in the U.S.A. No part of this book may be reproduced or copied in any form
without written permission from the copyright owner. GOLDEN BOOKS & DESIGN™, A GOLDEN
BOOK®, A LITTLE GOLDEN BOOK®, and the distinctive gold spine are trademarks of
Golden Books Publishing Company, Inc. Library of Congress Catalog Card Number: 96-75807
ISBN: 0-307-98786-8   A MCMXCVI   First Edition 1996

On the day before Christmas, the Dalmatian Plantation was a busy place. The one hundred and one Dalmatian puppies were very excited, for this would be their first Christmas.

The puppies watched as Nanny put some boxes beneath the tree. "What is she doing?" they asked their parents, Pongo and Perdita.

"Humans give presents at Christmas to show that they care about each other," Perdita explained.

"Let's give our humans a present," Lucky said.

"I know a great surprise!" Roly shouted. He fetched his best bone.

"Humans don't chew bones," Lucky said.

A little later the puppies went for a walk. They trotted down the path to the village green. Everywhere, they saw children playing in the snow.

"We could give our humans a ball," Penny said.
"I don't think Roger and Anita play fetch," Lucky answered.
"How about a dog blanket?" Freckles asked.
"We need a special gift," said Lucky, "but what?"
The puppies felt very discouraged.

But as he watched the children, Lucky had an idea. "I know a great gift we can make for our humans," he shouted. "Follow me!" He raced home with the others close behind.

When they reached the Dalmatian Plantation, Lucky started digging in the snow. "Watch me, and do what I do," he called to his brothers and sisters.

The puppies watched as Lucky rolled a big pile of snow into a ball.

"That looks like fun!" they shouted. Soon snow was flying everywhere.

From the snow ball, Lucky dug out a puppy with four legs. But just as he removed the last bit of snow from between the puppy's paws—WHUMP—it collapsed right on top of him.

"I guess my idea doesn't work," Lucky said, shaking snow from his ears.

"Let's make sitting-down puppies instead of standing-up puppies," Patch suggested. "Then maybe they won't fall down."

So, all afternoon, the little Dalmatians dug and rolled and scooped and scraped the snow into little snow puppy shapes. Freckles, Patch, and Penny found sticks for tails.

"Our puppies need eyes and noses," said Roly. "Let's use coal." He and the others ran to the shed and brought back shiny black lumps of coal.

Lucky looked at his snow puppy and frowned. "These puppies still don't look like us," he said. "Something else is missing. But what could it be?"

Then Lucky saw all the black paw prints leading from the coal shed across the snowy yard. "That's it!" he shouted. "Our puppies need spots!"

"Rub your paws in the coal dust," Lucky told the others.
"Then you can put black spots on the snow puppies."
Working busily, the Dalmatians covered their creations
with black spots.

Soon it was time to go inside.

After dinner, Nanny read the puppies a story about
Santa Claus and tucked them into bed. The puppies were
so excited, they wiggled and giggled for a long time.

At last they fell asleep. In their dreams, Santa Claus was
looking at their snow puppies. "Ho, ho, ho! What a fine
surprise!" they heard him say.

At last it was Christmas morning. Roger, Anita, and Nanny had given each puppy a ball, a bone, and a warm red sweater. The puppies loved their gifts, but they couldn't wait any longer to give their own.

The pups ran to the door and barked and barked.
"What's the matter with these puppies?" Nanny asked
Roger and Anita, as the dogs pushed and pulled them
out the door.

Finally they were outside. And then, when they looked around, Roger and Anita and Nanny began to laugh and cheer.

For there sat one hundred and one beautiful snow
puppies, with stick tails, black coal eyes and noses,
and—best of all—lots and lots of very black spots.

"Oh, you clever puppies!" Roger and Anita exclaimed
as the puppies proudly wagged their tails.

Nanny laughed so hard, she sat down right in the snow. "Why, that's one hundred and one of the best Christmas gifts I've ever had," she said, hugging as many puppies as she could hold.

And everyone agreed that it was so.